A THOUSAND WORDS

A Collection of Poems

& Short Stories

C E J WATERSON

In memory of my dear sister, Susan

who encouraged me to write

and chase my dreams

CONTENTS

A THOUSAND WORDS

"Write a thousand words," he said. "Write about anything you like."

But what one thousand words will I write? Deep, dark and meaningful or light and fluffy? What one thousand words will I choose? There are so many words to choose from, and with no defined topic, I can just write! So, should I write about what I know, or exercise my imagination? Maybe I should recall events from the past? There's plenty of those! It took me ten years to complete my memoirs and the final result is a tome that makes a very useful doorstop!

I began writing at a very young age, coming I think from my love of reading. My favourite place was the public library; an imposing double-fronted red brick building, surrounded by mature trees, weedless flower beds and immaculately manicured lawns. Its Georgian windows overlooked a lily pond where a weeping willow dipped its tendrils into the deep, clear water, providing a safe haven for ducks and moorhens. A bandstand stood at the heart of this beautiful park where, during the summer, lively music resonated throughout the neighbourhood.

I clearly remember the struggle I had to push open the heavy wooden door with its bright brass handle and enormous letterbox. I can still recall the smell of polish and the very shiny floor; standing on tiptoe to return my books to the librarian;

the sound of silence, only interrupted by murmured whispers and the thump of the date stamp. I was in my element, slowly browsing along the shelves, carefully selecting three books to take home.

We didn't have television and my sister was nearly nine years older than me, so not much of a playmate. I had friends, but was content in my own company and led quite a solitary, often imaginary, childhood. The horse I kept in the garage was cantered energetically around the garden, jumping obstacles erected from bamboo canes and wooden boxes. I flitted balletically through the apple trees or chatted to the little folk living in the coal shed. The garden was my magical place, where I could make anything happen!

If I couldn't get outside, then I liked nothing better than to curl up in a chair in front of the fire with a good book, or scribble away writing stories. I avidly read everything from cartoon strips in the daily newspaper to historical novels. Every wild adventure, mysterious happening or perilous war story could be that enthralling, I would hide the book under my pillow at bedtime to be retrieved later and read by torch light under the covers.

I didn't like school; except for English subjects, at which I managed to excel, but I was never the teacher's pet. When asked to produce an essay of no more than two pages, mine nearly always ran to more than twenty! I simply couldn't help it – words just flowed!

Stay with me, we're almost half way!

My last years at school were the best. I learnt shorthand and typing; both of which proved invaluable and not only enhanced my writing skills, but guaranteed I was never without a job. I worked as an administrator for the NHS for many years, in between being a Police Officer, Estate Agent, Florist and most recently, IT Trainer. I was a mum too and, looking after two lively boys, meant there was little opportunity to write creatively, but I sent long, newsy letters to my family and wrote pantomimes for the PTA.

When my husband set up his own business, we had to get computerised to keep up with demands from clients all over the world, which I fought against at first because everything seemed to take a lot longer. It was much quicker and easier for me to produce letters and invoices on an electric typewriter, than fiddle about inserting floppy discs. However, once computers advanced to having built-in hard drives, and software became more manageable with a mouse, we progressed and have never looked back. I'm still amazed at how easy it is to take a photo or create a document and, within minutes, print it out or send it whizzing through the ether to wherever it needs to be! Even more wonderful, is being able to chat to family and friends face-to-face, no matter where they are!

Many years ago, I enrolled on a course with Writer's Bureau, but other commitments hampered my progress and it wasn't until recently I was able to take it up again. I was excited at the prospect of finally attaining a diploma for something I really enjoyed doing. Unfortunately, my experience was short-lived as I found assignments too confining and the tutor's comments somewhat harsh. I'm more than willing to accept constructive criticism, but resent generic influences on my work.

Having been a member of several inspirational writing groups, I'm always delighted when any of my short stories or poems are selected for publishing or broadcasting on radio or the Talking Newspaper. One group, Word Weavers, produced an anthology about Finding Time, which was well received; as were our efforts in creating an on-line performance during lockdown. A second anthology is in the making, based-on Women's Voices.

I'm rarely lost for words, but writing is, more often than not, an escape from reality; a way of expressing my innermost thoughts. My father, a man of very few words, kept a diary from the age of fourteen, when he ran away to sea. Those little books were all that was left of him when he passed away and I had the notion to write his story, but my mother decided otherwise; she considered the contents too personal and burnt the lot!

Now, some of my grandchildren have shown a keen interest, especially in poetry, and nothing gives me greater pleasure than when they share their work, completely unfettered by age or status. Clearly, they've inherited my love for reading and writing, as well as incredibly good looks!

That's it folks! Exactly, one thousand words!

A CHRISTMAS STORY

It's Christmas Eve and, as if by magic, it starts snowing. Just a fine flurry at first, but gradually, the flakes get bigger and settle on the ground. Soon the garden is cocooned in a white blanket.

There's a tap at the window and Martha breaks a biscuit before opening it. A robin hops on to her finger and pecks at the crumbs before flying off to perch in the lilac tree; his bright red breast, a vibrant splash of colour against the paleness of the landscape. Martha listens to his cheerful song for a few moments, before closing the window against the chill.

She returns to her favourite chair, from where she can see all that is happening, which is rarely anything much, as she lives at the end of a quiet cul-de-sac. Today, it seems even more peaceful in the silence that follows a fall of snow.

The Postman opens the garden gate, looking for her as he does so, and gives her a wave. She waves back, but doesn't hurry to get up for the mail. He glances her way again as he shuts the gate behind him and gives her a 'thumbs up'. She's glad of his daily attention, especially as some days, he's the only person to visit.

His concern for her is touching, and she thinks back to when the postie delivered at Christmas to her home when she was a child. Her mother would invite him in to the hallway for a glass of sherry, where he'd stand on the doormat with the snow from his boots thawing into a puddle. Martha pondered now, whether every household offered similar sustenance, and just how tiddly would he be by the end of his round?

Her tabby cat leapt nimbly onto her lap and, after a little kneading, settled down. As she stroked the sleek fur, she fondly recalled other memories.

Stirring a wish into the pudding and then hiding silver threepenny pieces wrapped in greaseproof paper. How did no one ever choke or break a tooth? The tree, originally 'found' in a forest, was dug from the garden each year and soaked in a bucket of water until Christmas Eve, when it was ceremoniously planted in a tub and decorated. Excited children placed an empty sock at the end of their beds in the expectation of it being filled by morning. It always was; crammed full of little gifts, sweets and fruit to enjoy at whatever ungodly hour they awakened.

After breakfast, the family went to church, lustily singing carols and trailing passed the nativity. A late lunch of roast chicken, with all the trimmings, was followed by the Queen's speech before they were allowed to open presents from under the tree. The evening was spent playing silly games. What fun they had; so much laughter.

A thud on the window startled Martha and the cat. A snowball was slithering down the pane and she could hear laughing and chatter coming from the other side of the fence. Scooping the cat out of her lap, she hurried to the hallway and donned wellingtons and a warm jacket. On the doorstep, she grabbed a fistful of snow in readiness for retaliation, but when she peered into next door's garden, it was empty except for a snowman. Disappointed, she let go of the snowball and the curious robin fluttered down to her feet. His shrill chirping cheered her as she went back inside.

She was reading a newsy letter from her niece, when the doorbell rang. Answering it, she found her neighbour Tom, looking a little sheepish, with his two children.

"I've come to apologise; I'm afraid a snowball went astray and hit your window. I hope it didn't do any damage."

"No, not at all, just woke the cat!"

"I'm so sorry."

The children looked solemn too and little Suzie said, "Will you come and have Christmas dinner with us tomorrow?"

Before Martha could reply, Tom said, "We'd really like you to, unless you've got other plans?"

"I've nothing planned and I'd be delighted! Thank you, that's very kind."

"We'll probably eat about one thirty, but do come in earlier."

"I look forward to it."

The children went scurrying off to tell their mum and Tom said, "See you tomorrow," as he followed them.

Martha cheerfully waved as she shut the door, genuinely excited at the prospect. Tom and his family hadn't long moved in and, although they were always friendly and polite, they'd only chatted over the garden fence. This was her first proper invitation.

She was awake early and, with a feeling of anticipation she'd not experienced in years, set about making mince pies and a Yule log. She didn't want to go empty-handed.

By twelve o'clock, Martha was ready. She didn't need to knock as the children had been looking out and greeted her at the door.

"Merry Christmas," they chorused.

"Merry Christmas," Martha responded as she handed over the pies and cake to Rachel, their mum. Tom surprised her, by kissing her on the cheek under the mistletoe, as the children giggled. They led her into the living room, bright with fairy lights and sparkling tinsel. An enormous tree, ablaze with more lights and colourful baubles stood at the far end. Martha was admiring the decor when she became aware of another visitor, who Rachel introduced as George, her dad. Martha felt herself blushing as they shook hands. Tall and lean; still with a good head of grey hair and a smile that touched his eyes, Martha immediately warmed to his obvious charm.

"He's our grandad," announced Suzie. "Will you be our grandma?"

Martha was alarmed by this sudden turn of events and didn't quite know how to respond. George came to her rescue by saying, "Maybe just for one day?"

"OK, but you'll have to tell me what to do because I've never been a grandmother before!"

This seemed to amuse the children and they had a lot of fun getting her to play games and read them stories. The afternoon went quickly and when it was nearly their bedtime, Martha made the excuse that she must go and feed her cat. The children hugged her as they said, "Goodnight," and Suzie added, "thank you for being our grandma."

"Thank you for having me; I've had a lovely time. It's been the nicest Christmas I've had in ages."

Martha noticed George had his jacket on as he helped her into her coat, "I'll walk you home."

"I only live next door," Martha said laughing, missing the wink he gave Tom and Rachel.

George took Martha's arm as they walked the short distance to her house. At the door, he said, "Any chance of a cuppa?"

To her surprise, Martha found herself saying, "I'll put the kettle on," and led the way through to the kitchen.

Tabitha, the cat appeared and wrapped herself round George's legs, loudly purring.

"You're honoured," Martha said, "she's normally very wary of strangers."

"I hope we're not strangers Martha. Today you made an old man very happy, as well as the children."

"I'm glad and it made me happy too!"

They took their tea through to her cosy sitting room and sat chatting easily. George told Martha that sadly, his wife had died from cancer not long after Suzie was born, leaving a huge hole in their lives.

"Hence the request for a grandma." he said smiling.

"I'm so sorry George, I didn't realise. I hope I didn't upset anyone with my antics?"

"On the contrary Martha, you made our day! I was wondering if you'd have lunch at the pub with me tomorrow? Tom's brother and his family are coming for the day and it'll be bedlam."

"I'd like that very much, thank you."

"Good, that's settled then. I'll pick you up about twelve."

Martha went with George to the door, where he kissed her on the cheek as they said goodnight.

When he'd gone, Martha sat in her chair for a long time, re-living the day and realised that, for once, she wasn't reminiscing about the past, but wistfully thinking about the future.

A FAMILIAR FACE

As we shake hands, it's like looking at myself in the mirror. Her hair is long and blonde and mine dark and short, but everything else is uncannily similar. Hazel eyes, a little ridge on the nose, even the same smile!

Fascinated, I realise I'm staring and still holding her hand. I let go and desperately try to focus on what she's saying. Anna, her name is Anna and she's the Marketing Manager for the Company where I've recently been appointed as Head of Human Resources. The likeness is very obvious to me, but Anna doesn't seem to notice and takes me through to an open plan office to introduce me to her colleagues. I watch carefully, to see if there's any reaction; seeing us together and looking so alike. There's none.

Anna invites me to her office for coffee and I'm unnerved again when I see on her desk, in pride of place, a school photograph. My heart is pounding and it takes every ounce of control not to blurt out, "Where did you get that?" Instead, I take a deep breath and look again. Yes, it could have been my school photograph, but the uniform is different and I had plaits, not a pony tail.

"Is that your daughter?" I ask tentatively, "She looks very like you."

"Everyone says that poor girl. It's even worse now she's older, people think we're sisters!"

I manage to drag my thoughts back to the present and concentrate on talking about working relationships; pay and conditions and the future vision for the company, especially in Marketing. I finish my coffee and with as much composure as I can manage, I shake Anna's hand again and leave her office.

My legs are like jelly as I head back along the corridors to HR. What just happened? How could we look so similar and no one else notice or comment on it? I reach the sanctity of my office and thankfully shut the door.

My computer is on and blinking at me expectantly. I type in Anna's name. Instantly her details come up on the screen and right at the top, just below her name is her date of birth. 26th December, 1965 - the same as mine!

It's evening and I call my parents. As always, they're pleased to hear from me and naturally ask how I'm getting on in my new job. I'm able to say it's going well and after a few more pleasantries, ring off.

I dig out my birth certificate, which names my mother and father and states I was born in a nursing home, close to where my parents still live in Surrey. I don't know what other answers I expected to find, but wonder where Anna was born.

I take Mum up on her offer of Sunday lunch and drive out to our family home in the countryside. We're chatting amiably in the living room and I can't help scan the many photos displayed there. I've not really looked at them for years and wonder how I can do so without being obvious. I can't, so I tell them one of the managers at work went to my old school and pick up my school photo. The pose is the same, even the dark hair, but tied differently. I'm again stunned by the likeness.

Mum has retrieved her favourite photo. Clearly done professionally; I'm about six months old, happily smiling for the camera and holding my teddy bear.

"I've still got that little bear," I say wistfully.

Mum reminisces about how he was given to me when I was born. After a painful and difficult delivery, I'd been whisked away to an incubator as I was blue and hardly breathing. She didn't see me for two days.

I've heard this story a thousand times, but now it takes on more significance and I feel a growing sense of foreboding. There's a lump in my throat and a knot in my stomach as I struggle to speak without giving away my emotions. Dad asks me if I'm alright.

"You've gone awfully pale."

I reassure him I'm fine, just tired and don't argue when Mum suggests I stay the night. I sleep fitfully and keep going over and over everything in my mind. Anna looks a lot like me, so does her daughter; we have the same date of birth. So what? It doesn't prove anything.

Monday morning and I go straight to work. I'm trawling through e-mails and absentmindedly answer a tap on the half-open door. It's Anna. I greet her warmly and invite her to sit down. As she does so, I become acutely aware of yet something else I find hard to ignore. Barely concealed by make-up, a mole on her right cheek - exactly the same place as mine! I'm not sure if I gasp, but before I can say anything, she asks me if I've had a good weekend.

"Great thanks," I stammer, "I went to see my parents."

"So did I, well my mum anyway, I don't have a dad."

"I'm sorry," I say presuming he must be dead.

"Oh don't be, he left us before I was born. They weren't married and he went off with someone else as soon as he knew my mum was pregnant. We've not seen or heard from him since."

My training kicks in and I manage to commiserate and not give way to my mounting curiosity.

Without prompting, Anna continues, "We had to live with my grandparents when I was little. They've both passed away and Mum gets a bit lonely, so I go out to see her as often as I can."

"Where does she live?"

"Woking in Surrey."

My stomach lurches and my heart skips a beat and then I find myself quietly saying, "Do you have brothers or sisters?"

"No. It's just me and Mum."

I'm letting go of the breath I've been holding when Anna says, "I had a twin, but sadly she was still born."

I'm perilously close to losing it, but Anna doesn't seem to realise my distress and is apologising for keeping me. She'd come to make a request for a temp to help out with a backlog of admin, which I duly note and she leaves.

I go to the window and open it, taking in great gulps of fresh air. My mind is racing as I try to process this latest piece of information. With growing anguish, I realise my greatest fear is that somehow, I was swapped at birth. Anna's mum was a single parent. It was going to be hard for her to bring up one child, never mind two. My mum gave birth to a little girl, who maybe didn't survive.

Only DNA testing would prove my suspicions beyond doubt, but what would that achieve? My dear parents, who've loved and supported me my entire life, would be devastated if they knew their little daughter had actually died and I belong to someone else. What about Anna's mum? How would she react, learning her second baby didn't die after all and is still alive and well forty years later?

The consequences of knowing what might well be true could prove too overwhelming and nothing can change the events of the past. For now, at least, what I believe must remain a secret.

A SPIDER'S WEB

Lisa tapped in the code and waited for the click before opening the door. The building was quiet and there was no one in reception. She took the stairs, rather than the lift, to the second floor and was pleased to see there was no one here yet either. She needed a cup of coffee and a couple of paracetamols, to ease the headache she'd woken up with, before starting her day.

Dumping her bag at her desk, Lisa switched on the computer. By the time she'd made the coffee, the machine would have warmed up and kicked into life. It was always so slow on Mondays.

She was pouring water in to her mug when she heard familiar whistling. Dan - he was always so damn cheerful. "Hi Dan, do you want a coffee?"

Dan poked his head round the kitchen door with a look of surprise on his face, but Lisa didn't notice. "Hello you. How you doing?"

"Well thank you, except for a banging headache. It must have been one hell of a party at Deirdre's, but I'm ashamed to say I don't remember!"

Dan looked puzzled, but said, "You certainly looked as though you were enjoying yourself. I'll have that coffee please if you're offering. Did you get the milk?"

"Oh hell - is it my turn? I forgot - sorry."

"No worries, I'll get some before the others get in."

Lisa took her coffee black, so it was always hit and miss whether she would remember. She went back to her desk and stared at her in tray - it was almost empty. *That's impressive,* she thought, *I must have had a very good week to get most of that done.*

She heard the clip of heels coming along the corridor and knew it would be Marcia. She liked Marcia; they had worked together for five years now and always got along.

"Morning," Lisa called out, "kettle's boiled and Dan's just gone to get the milk as I forgot again!"

There was no response until Marcia stepped into the room. "Oh my god, it's you and I'm loving the new look!"

"Who were you expecting?" Lisa responded laughing.

"Well obviously your holiday did you good, you're very tanned unless that's fake?" Marcia teased.

Lisa hadn't realised she looked any different to how she usually looked. Her hands and arms were brown she now noticed and she was wearing a colourful summer dress that felt new.

Before they could say anything more, Dan's whistling was heard on his return from getting the milk and muted voices were coming from the kitchen.

"That'll be Robbie in," Marcia said looking at her watch. "Jenny's late, but she's been doing loads of overtime. I'll just grab a coffee, then we can have a catch up."

Lisa was beginning to feel uneasy, but couldn't figure out why. She was getting the impression from her colleagues that they hadn't seen her in a while; the reason being she'd been on holiday, only she couldn't remember! That party must have been some bash and she was hoping she hadn't made a fool of herself. Surely Marcia would tell her if she had?

Without having any more time to think about what might or might not have happened, Jenny appeared and walked straight passed Lisa's desk without saying a word.

"Morning," Lisa said with a smile. Jenny just glared at her and stomped back out of the office.

Lisa was really unnerved now and, determined to find out what was going on, headed for the kitchen where she could hear them all talking.

"Who does she think she is? Swanning in as if nothing's happened and looking like she's won the lottery!"

Jenny's outburst stopped Lisa in her tracks and she decided not to barge in nor eavesdrop further. She took a detour to the ladies' cloakroom. There she looked in the mirror. She did have a nice healthy glow and her hair was in a bob, but wasn't that how she always wore it? Honestly, she was going to have to give up drinking if she couldn't even recognise herself! She took a couple of deep breaths and splashed her face with water. Shakily she returned to the office and sat down at her desk, avoiding any eye contact or further conversation.

The phones started ringing and everyone was busy all morning. By lunchtime, Lisa was feeling a little more herself and took a walk to the park hoping that might clear her head.

It was a lovely summer day and, having strolled around the small lake admiring the water lilies and listening to the ducks chuckling, she found a seat. Closing her eyes, she let the heat from the sun calm her thoughts.

"Hello stranger," a voice said.

Lisa squinted into the sun, but couldn't tell who it was.

"Hello," she responded.

"May I sit down?"

Lisa moved over to make room. A tall, dark, handsome young man sat down beside her and putting his arm around her, gave her a hug and a peck on the cheek.

"How've you been?" he said, "I've missed you."

Lisa really didn't know what to say as she couldn't recall this person and yet she felt very comfortable in his presence.

"Well thank you, apart from a splitting headache. How's yourself?"

"I'm surprised you care. I'm afraid I didn't behave very well when we were last together. Have you forgiven me?"

As Lisa had no idea what this man had done, she had no idea whether she would have forgiven him or not, so she simply said, "Let bygones be bygones."

The man gave her another hug and said, "Perhaps we can meet up for a drink sometime soon?"

"I'm pretty busy right now, trying to catch up after a holiday."

"Of course - you must have quite a backlog if you've been away. Call me. I don't want to lose touch."

With that, the man stood up and, blowing Lisa a kiss, strode away.

Who the hell's that? Lisa asked herself. She rummaged in her handbag and found her phone. Scrolling through her contact list, she was hoping a name would leap out at her and she would remember, but there was nothing. Indeed, she wasn't sure she recognised many of the names listed. The screen went blank; it needed charging. She would have to leave further searches until she got home.

The afternoon was as frenetic as the morning and Lisa had no opportunity to speak to Marcia in the hope of shedding some light on her life, love or otherwise. She was still on a call when everyone was leaving for the night. All, but Jenny, waved goodbye and Marcia mouthed, "See you tomorrow," as she disappeared behind the others. Lisa felt strangely abandoned.

Five minutes later as she was switching off her computer and clearing her desk, a tap on the door announced her boss Robbie. "Good to have you back."

Impulsively Lisa asked, "How long have I been away?"

Robbie looked somewhat bemused and answered, "Just over a month. Why do you ask? Are you alright?"

Lisa didn't really know how to answer, but said, "I'm fine; I just feel as though I've been away a lot longer. I'm guessing Jenny's had to fill in for me and she's not very happy about it."

"Jenny's never very happy and yes she's done lots of overtime whilst you've been away and been well paid for it. Don't let her get to you. I don't mean to pry, but did you get your personal stuff sorted out?"

Again, Lisa had no idea what he was talking about, but valiantly said she had and thanked him for his concern.

She left the office in a daze. When she didn't find her car in the car park, she assumed she must have come in by bus and instinctively headed for the stop. She seemed to know where she was going, so how was it she had little or no memory about what else was happening?

By the time she entered her flat, she felt exhausted. What with the anxiety of not being aware of recent events and fielding complicated calls all day, she was shattered and still had a headache. She would have a cool shower in the hope she might feel reinvigorated and find a way of filling the gaps in her life without appearing stupid.

She tossed her handbag onto an armchair in the living room and plugged her phone in to its charger. She noticed two dirty glasses on the coffee table and an empty bottle of wine. Clearly that was the reason for her hangover this morning and ruefully she picked them up on her way to the kitchen. Here she found half a piece of toast and a mug still full of coffee, only there was a furry mould over everything as though it had been there for some considerable time.

Lisa stared at it all, unable to grasp how this had happened. She shook herself and put the toast in the bin and the coffee down the sink, almost retching with the smell. She went through to her bedroom. Surely here she would find everything as normal? To her dismay, the room looked as though it had been ransacked. There were clothes spilling out of drawers and the wardrobe doors were wide open. A suitcase was half packed or half emptied? Lisa simply didn't know!

She threw herself on the unmade bed in frustration. She just couldn't remember and was no nearer piecing together the jigsaw of the past few weeks. She heard the ping of her mobile as a message came in and despondently went to see what it was.

A text read 'Really good to see you today and do hope I'm forgiven. I want to make it up to you. Can we meet asap?' The sender was Tom.

Was that Tom she'd met in the park? It must be, but she still couldn't remember knowing him. What was she to do? Where had she been if not at home? Who would know or who could she ask?

She went to have a shower and was relieved to see the bathroom looking orderly, but then noticed a man's razor and another toothbrush next to hers. She couldn't ignore these signs because now she wondered if someone she didn't know (or couldn't remember) was likely to walk in unannounced.

She went back through the flat to the front door to make sure it was locked on the inside. Just as she was putting the chain across, the bell rang making her jump. Cautiously she opened the door and peered round it.

"Hi Lisa. It's me, Stella. Can I come in?"

Lisa instantly recognised her neighbour and gladly let her in. It seemed natural to hug and Stella said warmly, "So good to have you back. I've bought a bottle to celebrate."

She obviously knew her way to the kitchen and went to a cupboard for glasses. "You look great - that new hairstyle really suits you. Did you get it done in Cyprus?"

Is that where I've been? Lisa thought to herself.

"You've got a great tan," Stella went on as she poured the wine. "Cheers my dear!"

"Cheers," Lisa responded. "Will you tell me the truth Stella, if I ask you a silly question?"

"Depends what it is, but I expect so."

"What happened at Deirdre's party? Did I make an idiot of myself? I must have had too much to drink because I honestly don't remember, but I think I've been paying for it ever since."

Stella looked solemn for a moment then smiled kindly saying, "It was awkward with Richard showing up like that; you weren't expecting him and Tom got really jealous and went off in a huff. Richard was all over you and ended up here for the night. Sorry sweetie, but I saw him with you in the morning as you were leaving to go on holiday. He was putting your bags in his car and I assumed he was giving you a lift to the airport."

"I know this is going to sound crazy, but who is Richard?"

Stella looked at Lisa in amazement. "Your ex-husband or at least he will be when the divorce comes through. Are you OK? You're acting really weird and seriously worrying me now. What's happened?"

Lisa told Stella what she'd been through and admitted not remembering anything since Deirdre's party.

"That was weeks ago!" Stella exclaimed. "Where've you been since?"

"That's just it... I don't know!"

Stella thought for a moment and then asked Lisa to look on her phone. "Maybe you've taken photos or received emails or texts from people."

Lisa went through to the living room and disconnected her phone from the charger. She looked at her emails - nothing since the day before she went on holiday. No recent texts either, apart from the one from Tom. She swiped the photos and found only one. It was a 'selfie' with someone she didn't recognise. A blonde, curly haired young man with piercing blue eyes and a dazzling smile. She showed the photo to Stella.

"That's Richard, your husband. You don't recognise him, do you?"

Lisa shook her head in disbelief. *What's happening - why can't I remember?*

"You've obviously had a knock to the head or something and you've got amnesia," Stella said profoundly. "Maybe you should see a doctor."

"I've lost a few weeks of my life, but I'm not ill. A doctor would think I'm mad!"

"Perhaps you should get in touch with Richard and see what he says. You looked so loved up when you left and I did wonder if he was going to gate-crash your holiday. When you didn't turn up after two weeks, I honestly thought you'd gone back to him."

"Maybe I did, but I can't ask him, he'll think I'm loopy. What was I doing in Cyprus?"

"You were going to surprise an old school friend for her thirtieth birthday. Don't you remember that either?"

"No, but if it was to be a surprise and I wasn't there, she wouldn't miss me, but if I was there, surely I'd have photos?" Lisa took a deep breath and with a shrug of her shoulders said, "I don't know where I've been or who I've been with, but I'm obviously alright now, so maybe I should just forget what I can't remember!"

"I think you should get checked out," Stella said seriously.

"I'll sleep on it and see how I feel in the morning. Thank you."

The women hugged and Stella left Lisa to double-lock the door again. This was indeed a strange situation and one Stella wasn't sure would easily be resolved.

Lisa slept surprisingly well that night and woke feeling very much better. The headache had disappeared and she felt more able to cope. She still couldn't remember anything from Deirdre's party to yesterday morning, but it worried her less and with a cheerful determination, she got ready for work.

Her morning went pretty much the same as it had the previous day with everyone either engaged on calls or entering data. Jenny still wasn't speaking to her, but looked less hostile and the others showed concern, without being intrusive.

At lunchtime Lisa walked to the park again, wandering round the lake to sit on a bench in the sun. Her phone pinged to get her attention and she retrieved it from her handbag. It was a video message. She pressed play and was immediately disturbed to see who it was - the now recognisable, Richard. He was smiling and his eyes seemed to penetrate her very soul. She wanted to snap the phone shut, but found she couldn't. She was mesmerized and compelled to listen to him.

"Lisa, I did love you, but I don't want to keep you, so I'm letting you go. I'm freeing the butterfly from the spider's web. Au revoir."

Lisa stared at the screen, initially stunned and unable to comprehend the message, but then a realisation dawned and without further hesitation, she hurled the phone into the lake.

"That's a bit drastic!" a voice said behind her.

She turned to see Tom.

"I'm throwing away old memories to make way for new ones. Can we have that drink?"

EASTER TREATS

Mary drew the curtains and was relieved to see bright sunshine and a clear blue sky. She had a very busy day ahead and the decent weather would make all the difference.

She made a pot of coffee and some toast, which she took into the conservatory. She sat revelling in the glorious Spring day; clumps of primroses and daffodils reflected the brightness of the sun as it glistened on the little stream gurgling its way through the garden. A couple of ducks waddled up the lawn looking for crumbs from the bird table, and a rabbit was enjoying a tasty snack.

The chiming of the clock reminded her there was much to do and reluctantly she returned to the kitchen. Tidying away as much as she could, would give the ladies from the WI plenty of space to sort out their picnic. Their generously kind offer was greatly appreciated, leaving her free to organise everything else.

Collecting two full shopping bags from the hallway, Mary made her way across the road to the church. She slid the key from her pocket and opened the big heavy door. Inside it was cool, but with the sunshine flooding in, felt bright and welcoming. The only stained-glass windows were above the altar; the others being clear, allowing in the natural light. Beautifully arranged flowers everywhere made the church look 'dressed' for the occasion and Mary took a moment to breathe in their heady scent, pleasantly disguising the normally musty smell of the old building.

Mary had been at the church since Christmas, taking over from the Minister who'd been there for many years and was now retired. In the heart of the Scottish Highlands, it was a delightful spot, surrounded by pine forests and bordering the banks of the River Spey. Coming from a bustling seaside town to this sleepy hamlet had been a culture shock for Mary, but in a good way.

Of the three villages in the Parish, only two still had a church; the third one sadly having become a ruin. The main Church, in the town five miles away, always had a good-sized congregation and Mary was required to assist at Holy Communion and special Festivals. There, formalities were strictly observed and traditions upheld. She'd enjoyed the pomp and ceremony of midnight mass, but had been totally enthralled at the family service on Christmas Day in her village.

There was a good turnout and the old Minister had surprised the congregation by telling jokes and performing a 'rap' to deliver his Christmas message, which in his Scottish accent, was highly amusing! Clearly, he was going to be a hard act to follow!

Even so, Mary had been dismayed when only a few people attended the first service of the new year. She shook hands with them all as they left and got the distinct impression this occurrence was nothing unusual. She tried hard not to be paranoid about being a female and not being a local, but this was perplexing and she vowed to find out the reason.

She'd called her predecessor, now living on the Black Isle, and asked him if he could shed any light on why this had happened. He immediately explained that at Christmas, family members of the Estate, the workers with their families and any visitors, were expected to attend Church. He'd also expanded on the dynamics of the village; mainly consisting of just two families with only a smattering of incomers. Over the years, the church-going population had shrunk through demise or moving away and the modern generation had the notion that church was only for the gentry. He'd apologised for not enlightening Mary, but felt it was better for her not to have any preconceived ideas. She'd thanked him for the information and rang off, determined to somehow improve the situation.

Firstly, she'd decided if the people wouldn't come to her and to the Church, then she would have to go to them. The Community Hall was always busy and she knew this would be the place to start. Recently a cafe had been opened there and she was keen to meet the people who used it. The two ladies doing the catering were very friendly and chatted about everyone. Seemingly, the vast majority of customers were lorry drivers, who found it a convenient stop on their way through in their huge tankers bound for whisky distilleries or taking logs to timber yards. A few locals used it regularly, but not many.

Mary had gone incognito, without her dog collar, but the ladies seemed to know who she was and were curious about her. She'd been completely open and honest with them and in return, they'd given her information, enabling her to piece together what life was really like in their rural community.

She'd made almost daily visits to the café, chatting to anyone who happened to be there and discovering how the people in this part of the world liked to live. Clearly there was a mountain to climb in her bid to increase the numbers in her congregation, but she was more than willing to listen and find ways to compromise.

In between hospital and home visits to the sick and elderly, she'd found time to do what the locals did. She became a member of the indoor bowling club; she joined the WI (or the Rural as its better known in Scotland); she supported Whist Drives and Quiz Nights; she helped out with the local play group and visited schools. Soon she became a familiar figure in the town and villages and, little by little, support for her and the Church had grown.

Today, she was hosting a family fun day for the first time. The Easter Sunday service was to be for anyone who wanted to come. She'd invited the congregations from the Church in town and the other villages and had been pleasantly surprised by the positive reaction with many offers of help. In particular, one young man named Josh, had not only offered to play the organ for the service, but also provide live music on his keyboard throughout the afternoon.

Mary busied herself tucking Easter eggs of all shapes and sizes into many of the nooks and crannies, making some more obvious to find than others. She didn't think children rummaging around was sacrilegious at all, it would be just wonderful to have people enjoying themselves in Church. She arranged crayons and colouring books at the back of the church to amuse the children during the short service.

She was pleased with her efforts and returned to the Manse to find the Rural ladies already laying out their dainty sandwiches, tray bakes and fancy cakes.

A duck race was being set up, by one of the 'ghillies' from the Estate, and he was in his waders, strategically placing netting in the stream to stop the plastic ducks from bobbing into the river.

She could hear cars parking up and excited children's voices. As she went to greet them, Mary just knew this was going to be a very special day.

ELOISE

I know exactly who this young lady is that's just entered the salon. Last week my colleague interviewed several girls from the local college for our junior position and from her description, this is Eloise.

"Good morning, may I help you?" I say as I want to see how she introduces herself.

"I'm Eloise Brown," she mumbles, hiding her face behind a curtain of mousey-brown hair.

"Welcome Eloise, it's nice to meet you." I extend my hand and hesitantly Eloise returns the gesture, giving me a glance through one black-kohled eye. Her clasp is limp and there's no enthusiasm. Oh dear, this is going to be hard work.

Before I can say anything more, Daisy, our newest recruit, appears to take over desk duties. I introduce them and it's very noticeable how different they are. On Daisy's first day, she was full of confidence and chatter; Eloise is barely able to say a word.

I take her through to the staff room and introduce her to the other stylists who are getting ready for a busy day. The girls, Beth and Kimberly greet her warmly and Sean goes in for a hug. He's very camp and very funny and I see a glimmer of a smile from Eloise. Good, that's who I'll put her with once I've shown her the ropes.

The others go through to the salon and I invite Eloise to sit down and tell me about herself. I need to know why she's so painfully shy.

"What are you expecting to learn here?" I ask.

"Hairdressing," she replies rather sullenly.

"What are your hopes and dreams?"

"I dunno really."

"Well, what's your ambition? What would you really like to do for a living?"

"Hairdresser or make-up artist for films or TV."

Really? I find that hard to believe, but hopefully as we get to know her better, she'll open up and become more self-assured.

"Let's make that happen then Eloise."

I give her a tunic, the same as the others, with our embroidered logo on it and I'm pleased to see she's wearing black trousers as instructed.

"Would you mind tying your hair back?" I ask kindly. "You'll need it out of your eyes when you're in the salon."

Eloise looks at me fearfully for a second, but rummages in her bag and finds a hairband. I leave her to change while I check on the day's appointments and make sure everyone knows what they're doing.

When I return to the staff room, I find Eloise sitting at the table, nervously biting her nails. Her hair is in a scruffy ponytail and I can see now she has a few adolescent spots on her chin under the pale Goth make-up and her ears protrude ever so slightly.

"That's better," I say encouragingly, "now I can see you properly."

Eloise visibly squirms under the scrutiny and I quickly move on to showing her what to do.

Her first job every day will be to empty the dryer of clean towels and fold them in a certain way before stacking them on shelves in the salon. The stylists like to sort their trays out themselves, but the junior is expected to sweep up between customers and make sure the chairs are free of hair. She'll be responsible for keeping the shampoo and conditioner bottles topped up and the sinks spotlessly clean. She'll be asked to make teas and coffees constantly throughout the day. Generally, she's a 'gofer', but there are perks. She can regularly have a free cut and blow dry and, although I didn't say it, a free manicure once her nails are long enough. Formal training will continue at college once a week and she'll be given plenty of opportunities to practise her skills.

I want her to use her initiative, but realise she may need some encouragement. Quietly, I ask everyone to include her in what they're doing whenever they can and by lunchtime, I'm already seeing a difference. She doesn't appear quite so nervous. Daisy especially, taking her more senior role very seriously, has been happily showing her what to do.

As expected, Sean has been brilliant. He loves an audience and had Eloise helping him with a perm and a complicated colouring.

I've had her taking customers' coats and helping them gown, which I thought might be a step too far, but after a bit of fumbling, she worked it out and was rewarded with a tip from two of our regulars.

I've been pleasantly surprised and impressed by her willingness to tackle even the most mundane tasks and despite her timid start, can see she could have a very bright future with us. I do hope so.

EMILY

The museum was quiet, having closed for the day. Julian had his coat on, ready to leave, but took a moment to look at one of the oil paintings he'd just received for restoration. It wasn't very big, but was very dirty and he could hardly make out what was beneath the grime. It looked like a young girl, but it was impossible to see her features or what she was wearing, so he had no real idea of period. It was likely to be Victorian as he'd restored quite a few paintings from the same place; a grand old house being lovingly renovated with no expense spared.

It was good business for Julian as the museum was small and non-profit making. True, the overheads were fairly modest as he was the curator as well as sole restorer and he was fortunate enough to have several very reliable volunteers to help with the guided tours. It was winter, so the museum had been quiet and it was a good opportunity for him to devote his time to his passion for restoring old paintings.

Julian switched off the powerful angle-poised lamp, looking forward to seeing what this little portrait would reveal over the coming days. He went round switching off lights and locking doors before finally setting the alarm and letting himself out into a chilly night.

Next morning, Julian was in early and the first thing he did was to take another look at the oil painting sitting on his bench. Switching on the powerful lamp and fixing the attached

37

magnifying glass, he examined the piece carefully. Even though it was filthy, he could tell it was a good work of art and was impatient to start its restoration.

He made himself a coffee and welcomed in the solitary volunteer who would be his only companion for the day. An elderly lady, Edith was very knowledgeable about all the exhibits and her enthusiasm was infectious. He would enjoy having her around and knew he could leave her to dust the cabinets and tidy shelves, generally making herself useful while he got on with the restoration.

Julian carefully removed the very grubby gilt frame and its backing and put them aside whilst he looked even closer at the picture itself. He could instinctively feel that it was fragile, the canvas being almost paper thin. This was going to be a very delicate operation.

He gently brushed away the surface dust and began painstakingly applying the cleaning fluid with a cotton wool swab. Little by little, doing a tiny piece at a time, the picture was gradually being revealed. His gestures were methodical and very thorough, paying great attention to detail. It was easy for Julian to become completely absorbed in what he was doing and he was very surprised when Edith popped her head round the door to say she was leaving.

"Good heavens is that the time?" He got up to see Edith out, "See you next week?"

"I wouldn't miss it for the world."

Julian locked the door behind her and put the closed sign up. He still had a couple of hours before he needed to leave and was anxious to get back to his project.

Only a quarter of the painting had been cleaned, but already he could see a big difference. This was going to be very satisfying when it was finished. Julian had a good look at the frame and spent the rest of the afternoon with a toothbrush and old towel, removing most of the dirt. It was never going to be as good as new, but then it shouldn't be - it was antique. He put the ornate frame to one side and studied the painting again. Looking for a signature, Julian couldn't find one, but maybe it would appear tomorrow.

He went through his routine of switching off lights, locking doors and setting the alarm before heading home.

Another volunteer, Alistair was waiting patiently for him to open up the next day. Apologising for keeping him waiting, Julian let them in to the museum. Switching on lights as they went through, Julian noticed a chill in the air and thought the heating probably hadn't come on. Alistair offered to make the coffees and Julian went to investigate. He was astounded to find a window open in his workshop, letting in the cold air, but otherwise the room was as he'd left it.

"How weird," he thought and, going through to the kitchen, said to Alistair, "I know I didn't leave that window open; it's been too cold. How very odd."

Julian left Alistair to look after the museum and went back to his workshop to make sure everything was still there. If there had been a thief, the alarm would've gone off and he'd have been summoned by the Police. It was very strange and made him feel uneasy.

He looked carefully through the works of art leaning against the walls and was relieved to find nothing missing. He turned his attention to his bench and could see the little painting was where he'd left it; *but then who would take a canvas in the middle of restoration*? Switching on his light and fixing the magnifying glass, he immediately saw in the opposite corner to where he'd cleaned, a tiny signature.

Julian was seriously doubting himself. Had he stayed to do this little piece last night after all? He remembered being curious, but was certain he'd decided to leave it. He felt the hairs on the back of his neck stand up and had the sensation that someone was watching him. To shake off the feeling, he joined Alistair in the museum, but didn't say any more about what he'd found.

Julian spent the rest of the morning trying to find a logical explanation and convince himself that somehow the window had blown open and the cleaning fluid had dribbled onto that part of the painting without him noticing. By lunchtime, with some trepidation, he was ready to take another look.

The painting was as he'd left it, but the signature had disappeared. Julian quickly decided he must have imagined seeing it and pulling himself together, prepared to resume the restoration. He worked on it meticulously, but felt an urgency to get it finished.

By the time Alistair came to tell him he was leaving, Julian had made good progress and over half the painting had been cleaned. The dress of the model was a deep blue and looked like velvet. Both men admired the artwork it took to produce that effect. Decisively, Julian snapped off his lamp and made sure the window was secure before completing his routine. He wasn't going to stay on today.

The next morning, Julian found himself hoping that whoever was volunteering was waiting for him, but there was no one at the door. He let himself in and went through the ritual of turning off the alarm and switching on lights. Nothing untoward, but he braced himself before entering his workshop. He was relieved to see the window was shut and putting the lamp on, found the painting exactly as he'd left it. Feeling more confident now, he set out the cotton wool swabs and cleaning solution in readiness to complete the project.

Julian made himself a coffee, wondering as he did so, where today's volunteer was, but as the museum was very quiet, he could manage on his own. He returned to his workshop and noticed the light flashing on the landline. Pressing play, he heard a croaky voice apologising, but they wouldn't be along today due to a heavy cold.

"Hey ho," Julian thought, "I'll muddle along, but will need to be in the museum in case someone comes in."

He busied himself for most of the morning rearranging a few of the artefacts and when he'd had no visitors by midday, put the closed sign up and a notice directing anyone wanting access to ring the bell.

Intending to complete the restoration of the little painting, Julian settled himself at his bench. He was about to uncover the face of the portrait and it made him nervous. Carefully as always, he applied the cleaner, left it for a few minutes before swabbing it off and buffing with a cloth. Within minutes, Julian had uncovered the cherubic features of a young child. Younger than he'd first thought as the Victorians tended to dress their children in the same fashion as themselves, but this little girl was no more than eight or nine years old. She had lively blonde curls framing a very solemn face. Her eyes were full of sadness, her mouth turned down, as though she were about to cry. Julian felt moved by what he saw and again was overcome by a feeling of disquiet.

"Who are you?"

"Emily," a voice whispered.

Julian couldn't be sure he'd heard it and looked about searching for the sound. He looked again and saw the rosebud lips mouth, "I'm Emily."

Thoroughly spooked, Julian snapped off his lamp, grabbed his coat and hastily went through his lock up routine before heading out into the winter's night. For once he was glad of the biting wind and the first flurry of snowflakes, pulling him out of his reverie as he hurried home.

He had a fairly sleepless night, so was mightily relieved to see not one, but two volunteers waiting for him. He felt the chill as soon as he opened the door and hastily made his way through the museum, fearing what he might find. Again, the window was open, but nothing was out of place and no damage done.

Feeling relieved and strangely calm, Julian shone his lamp on the painting and couldn't help but admire the clever brushstrokes that gave the little figure life. Smiling, he said, "What have you been up to Emily?"

Barely perceptible, he saw her smile. A shiver went down his spine and he resolved to return the painting as soon as possible.

Fetching the gilt frame and the wooden backing, both now in a presentable state, Julian was ready to put it all back together. He laid the frame face down and carefully put the painting in place, then the backing and as he did so, noticed an inscription, which read:

Emily Rose taken by the angels

Rest in peace my dearest child

Julian stared at the words through teary eyes and wondered why he hadn't seen it before. It must have been on the underside of the backing and he wondered whether to return the painting with the inscription concealed or reverse it to show the owner. He decided on the latter and completed the task he'd set out to do. Carefully enclosing the painting in bubble wrap, he noticed that Emily was still smiling.

Leaving the museum in the capable hands of the volunteers, Julian drove out to the stately home where the painting had been found. He wouldn't normally make a personal delivery, but somehow, he felt responsible and wanted to make sure the painting got back to where it belonged.

The owners were at home and delightedly welcomed him, anxious to see the painting restored. They were clearly very pleased with the results and intrigued when Julian showed them the inscription. Reading it, the lady of the house was almost ecstatic as she'd discovered a journal belonging to a Mabel Elizabeth Marchant referring to her only daughter, Emily Rose, sadly dying from tuberculosis.

Julian felt a lump in his throat, but couldn't bring himself to share his experiences. The couple came to their own conclusion that Emily's mother had written the little script in homage to her daughter and thanked Julian for all his efforts.

On his way back to the museum, Julian mused over the happenings of the last few days and wondered whether the whole episode had been purely a figment of his imagination.

FROM RAGS TO RICHES

The washing was billowing on the line against a grey, cloudy sky. Dot was keeping a wary eye on the weather as Bill would need his good shirt this evening.

Dot was excited. This was the first time they'd been to the Palais for years and she was really looking forward to it. Her hair was screwed up in rags under a headscarf and she'd found a lipstick in her best handbag. Clothes were still on rationing, but she'd managed to make a stunning dress from a pair of red and gold brocade curtains she found at a jumble sale. A neighbour had lent her a pair of strappy gold sandals. Bill's tuxedo was a little tight around his middle, but it would have to do.

Dot untangled the knots from her hair and shook out the curls. She was delighted with the effect and when Bill saw her, he smiled and said, "Cinderella, you shall go to the ball."

It was a fine night and good to be out walking in the full glare of street lamps. Bill and Dot joined other revellers as they made their way to the ballroom. The feeling of freedom was exhilarating, making everyone very happy. No more siren warnings of imminent air raids and hunkering down in shelters. The war was over and it was time to celebrate!

IT'S THE LITTLE THINGS

He's yelling at me uncontrollably; full of resentment. I can imagine his face puce with rage, spittle at the corners of his mouth. I certainly hadn't intended making him this angry and deeply regret mentioning his indiscretion.

Our relationship has been over for a while, but every so often he phones, usually when he's drunk, to ask how I am. I don't think he really wants to know, he's just lonely and needs someone to talk to. I've always been a good listener and as long as I agree with whatever he's saying, it's fine and usually lasts about ten minutes.

Today though, he's ranting about work, about politicians, about one of his ex-girlfriends and I've had enough! I tell him, in no uncertain terms, that I'm not interested in his problems or opinions anymore. He's immediately wheedling and apologetic; saying how much he still misses me and how sorry he is that we've broken up. This last comment makes me furious and I remind him that he left me for someone else. Instantly he's on the attack, accusing *me* of being utterly impossible to live with and it was all *my* fault that we'd split up!

When he'd left, I'd been too hurt to retaliate or ask why, and for weeks I kept hoping he'd come back. I still had feelings for him and I suppose that's why I kept taking his calls. Now, I stab at the red button and put my phone on silent!

I can't stop the tears rolling down my cheeks and go to the bathroom to find a tissue. I look in the mirror and tell myself it's over - all over - for good! Then I notice the toothpaste and can't help smiling. It's hard to believe now, but we rarely argued when we were together and when we did, it was over the little things like him taking the last of the toothpaste or putting an empty cereal packet back in the cupboard.

It's the weekend and I have to distract myself from constantly looking at my phone or worse, being tempted to answer it. Sorting through the drawers of my dressing table, I discover an old envelope. The postmark is Amsterdam. I thought I'd long since thrown this letter away, but obviously must have decided to keep it. I stare at it. I don't need to open it; I remember its contents only too well.

I rip it in half and then tear it again and again and again until it's in tiny pieces, like confetti. With satisfaction, I scoop it all up and take it to the bathroom where I throw it down the toilet, firmly pulling the chain. That letter, those words were from another life, another love that got lost. I survived that didn't I? Time to move on and live again.

LEAVING HOME

"I'm leaving," Joe said quietly.

"Leaving where?" his mother said distractedly, not looking up from the sewing she was doing.

"Home."

Liz looked up then and peered at her son over the rim of her glasses.

"Why?"

"It's time, I can't stay here forever."

Why not? Liz thought, but then recalled something her sister had said when her eldest left home.

"You bring them into the world, give them roots to grow and wings to fly."

Easier said than done. It had been hard enough to let go when Elspeth got married, but David had still been alive then; this was going to be tough. Now she would be on her own. She knew she was being selfish, but she loved having Joe around. He wasn't always at home, but knowing he was coming in and out was a comfort and she felt needed.

"A few of us are renting a house."

"Where?" It was like getting blood out of a stone and she could tell he was really uncomfortable discussing the situation.

"Watford."

Obviously somewhere had already been found and, with a heavy heart and swallowing the lump in her throat, she asked him when he was going.

"Next weekend, but Mum it's not far away and I'll be over to see you often."

"No doubt at mealtimes or when you've got washing to be done." She managed a smile then and he kissed her cheek before heading out to spend the evening with his mates.

Left alone Liz sobbed. Big tears dropping on to the curtains she was making. How was she going to cope? She dabbed at her eyes and blew her nose before finishing the seam she'd been doing.

"This is ridiculous," she scolded herself. "He'll be a few miles away, not the other side of the world!"

She carefully folded the material and switched off the machine. She'd done enough today. Her back was aching and she needed a bath. Upstairs, as she ran the water, her thoughts turned to the past and she tried to concentrate on all the happy times they'd had as a family. So often, in the middle of the night, she could only think of the sadness and the loss of people dear to her.

The warmth of the water soothed her and she closed her eyes contemplating what she would do without Joe. Determinedly she convinced herself she wasn't going to be a victim. She just had to figure out a way of not always being alone. She wasn't without friends, but quite a few had moved away when they retired and even though she'd been invited, she hadn't visited any of them.

That was the first revelation - now she would be free to do whatever she pleased. The feeling was alien and she knew it would take a while to get used to this liberation.

Years ago, they'd had a motor home and although she knew she wouldn't be confident driving a large vehicle, she thought a small campervan would be fun. When the children were little, they'd had a dog, but the devastation of having their pet put to sleep was so overwhelming, they'd not had any other. Now Liz was thinking she would give another dog a home and have company on her travels.

She was looking forward to the adventure.

LOST TIME

Rosie didn't often get official looking mail in the post, as most of her correspondence was done on-line. She checked the name and address in the window of the envelope, to make sure it was for her, before opening it. The headed paper bore the names Smithson, Briggs and Carter, a firm of solicitors. The letter was brief and formal, requesting she make an appointment at her earliest convenience to discuss a matter in respect of their client, Hugh Williams (deceased).

Who was Hugh Williams? She'd never heard of him before. What could they possibly want to discuss? Only one way to find out.

The reception area was cool, but Rosie felt uncomfortably hot and clammy as she sat on the edge of an old leather chair, flicking through the pages of Tatler. A smartly suited middle-aged man appeared and smiling, beckoned her into his office. He introduced himself as Phil Carter and warmly shook her hand. The surroundings felt surprisingly welcoming and the solicitor gestured for Rosie to take a seat. On his desk was a small package and she could see it was addressed to her. He followed her gaze and thanked her for coming.

"You must be wondering what this is all about, so I'll come straight to the point. My client, Hugh Williams, sadly died a month ago and since then the family have been sorting out his belongings. They've come across some information they think you should know."

"But I've never heard of him, so what's it got to do with me?" Rosie asked, somewhat abruptly.

"All will become clear when you open this package, but as the contents will be unexpected, it may help if I give you some background."

"Hugh Williams was a Captain in the Army during the war and was away for most of it. Just before he was sent abroad, he had a liaison with Elizabeth Davies, who I believe was your mother?"

"My mother's maiden name was Davies. She was known as Betty." Rosie replied cautiously.

"Quite so, but the relationship didn't last long and they didn't keep in touch, except for one letter. They both married and had families, although I think I'm right in saying that you're an only child?"

Rosie nodded saying, "How do you know all this?"

"When the family came to me with the contents of this package and the information they'd uncovered, I did some research before I was satisfied that what they found could be true."

"What is it?" Rosie whispered nervously.

"Captain Williams was your father."

"That can't be right - my dad was John Edwards - he's on my birth certificate."

"He undoubtedly is - Mr Edwards knew all about your mother's relationship with Captain Williams, but willingly agreed to become your father." Tapping the package, Phil Carter went on gently, "The letter in here explains it all. Would you like to read it?"

"I think I'd better because at the moment, none of this makes any sense," Rosie said desperately.

Rosie took the package and with trembling hands opened it, pulling out an old envelope, creased and yellowed with age; a tattered pocket diary and a very expensive looking Rolex watch. Rosie stared at the items lying in her lap. The only thing she recognised was her mother's writing on the envelope. Carefully and very tentatively she removed the letter within.

Dated 12th September 1940 she had written:

My dear Hugh,

I trust this will find you safe and well. I had hoped we could meet once more before you left, but fate has prevented that from happening. I have something to tell you, that would have been better said in person as it may come as a shock. I'm pregnant. I know we didn't mean it to happen, but it has. Our relationship was brief, but I like to think meaningful. I went to your house to tell you, but your mother said you'd already been called up. She also told me that you'd become engaged.

Consequently, I kept my condition secret until I met a wonderful man who cares enough about me to take our baby as his. We're soon to be married and I have no doubt at all that he will make a good husband and father.

It seems only right you should be made aware of what's happening, but as I don't know where you are or when you're likely to be back, I can only hope you will agree this is best for everyone.

I wish you and your fiancé all good wishes for the future.

Yours, Betty

Rosie's hands were still shaking as she tried to comprehend what she'd just read.

"How is this possible?" she asked, her eyes full of tears. "Mum was right, my dad was a good husband and father. He never gave me any reason to think I wasn't his and even though I know that's mum's writing and I've read what she's written, I can't believe it."

"In the diary there, Captain Williams mentions your mother and the occasions when they met. He also writes an entry on the day he received the letter, just before Christmas when he has to consider keeping his distance."

"What about the watch?" Rosie asked bewildered.

"The family want you to have it as a keepsake. They'd also like to meet you, but realise that maybe a step too far."

"I would've loved to have brothers or sisters when I was growing up," Rosie said wistfully. "Since my parents died, I thought I had no one, but now maybe I have."

"Captain Williams had three children with his late wife, two daughters and a son. They're nice people and I think you'll like them. It's a lot for you to take in and maybe you should take time to think about it, as inevitably, it will change your life.

Perhaps you'll get back to me in a day or two and let me know what you think?"

Rosie got to her feet somewhat unsteadily and when asked if she would like a cup of coffee, politely declined and after shaking hands again, headed for home.

Once there, Rosie sat in her cosy living room with the contents of the package laid reverently on the coffee table. She still couldn't quite believe what she'd discovered and went through feelings of perplexity, even anger at the deception, to pure elation at the thought of having an extended family. What should she do?

She read her mother's letter again and carefully trawled through the little leather diary to find the entries describing their times together. It had been a brief, but passionate affair and not without concern for one another given the imminence of war.

As Rosie read more from the daily accounts of Hugh Williams, she got a real sense of the man. His handwriting and the words written gave an impression of a quiet determination and someone reliable. There was a softer, more sensitive side to him as well and a good sense of humour. Rosie liked him and smiled at the irony when she saw that he'd received her mother's letter on 22nd December 1940, the day she was born. The entry for the next day confirmed his decision not to have any further contact, respecting my mother's unsaid, but very obvious wishes.

There was a lump in Rosie's throat as she closed the little book and put it to her cheek, taking comfort from its smoothness and imagining the feel of his hand. She picked up the watch, appreciating its quality and recognising the symbolic gesture made by the family. So much lost time. She wouldn't want to change the past, but welcomed the unexpected opportunity to share the future. She made the call.

ONE WOMAN'S WAR

The ominous sound of the siren was just audible above the thrum and clatter of the machines. One by one the women made their way calmly to the exit, switching everything off as they went and grabbing their coats and gas masks before heading outside. With everyone going in the same direction, the pace quickened to reach the shelter before the bombing began.

"Last one in shut the door!" came the command from within as all the workers, mostly women, moved through the tunnel to take a seat on rough benches.

"You'd think we'd be used to this by now," Lizzie said as she folded a blanket she found on the floor.

"It never gets any less scary," responded her neighbour. "I'm just glad me kids aren't here."

"Have you heard how they're getting on?" Lizzie asked.

"Seem to be doing alright. They loves the animals they do. I don't think they're missing me or their dad and probably won't want to come home!"

A dull thud and shudder, immediately followed by a deafening explosion, halted the conversation and at the sound of rubble being strewn in all directions, most of the occupants automatically put their hands over their ears and bent forwards in an attempt to shut out what was happening. The shelter withstood the detonation, but in the dim, flickering light, pale faces were etched with fear as they waited for the next onslaught.

An eerie silence filled the shelter; as if everyone within it, were holding their breath. Some had their eyes tight shut, murmuring prayers and wringing their hands. Some clung together, seeking comfort from one another and others simply stared beyond their present existence, their hopelessness palpable.

The drone from a doodlebug got louder and faded, thankfully passing low overhead before detonating. Further eruptions could be heard and shudders felt as more bombs were dropped on the surrounding neighbourhood. The women in the shelter huddled together, gripping each other for support. An eerie quietness descended once again; no one daring to speak.

This was nearly always a nightly occurrence, when most people were in their beds. The women in the shelter were the night shift at the munitions factory. Were it to take a direct hit, this bunker would not be a safe place at all and constantly being on high alert was taking its toll; signs of fatigue were evident.

Scarves tied into turbans kept their hair out of the machinery and most of them wore men's overalls, rolling up the sleeves and trouser bottoms. Their hands were calloused by the hard graft and nails were bitten to the quick. Sulphurous chemicals, used in the making of the ammunition, turned their skin yellow, earning them the nickname of 'canary girls'.

Time passed without further disruption, but no one moved to get back to work. They would wait for the 'all clear' before leaving the shelter. Whispered conversations began; murmurings of reassurance; even someone softly humming. Others quietly joined in and the tension gradually eased.

Eventually, the warden's whistle could be heard followed by the welcome sound of the siren, signalling there would be no more raids tonight. The women left the shelter, stretching their limbs and wrapping their coats around their thin bodies as they made their way back inside the factory.

"Thank God that's over," Lizzie said as she returned to her bench and started up her machine. There was something oddly comforting about the clank and jangle as the workings whirred into life again. It wouldn't be long before daybreak and the end of her shift, but she didn't particularly look forward to going home. There was always a chance it wouldn't be there, having been demolished during the night; all her worldly possessions gone. Even if it was still standing, it wouldn't be that welcoming. There would be no fire in the grate or meal on the table.

Before the war, she'd made sure her family came home to all those things; hugging each one as they returned, much to the annoyance of her teenage son, Billy, who called her soppy! Her husband, Jack, had enlisted into the Army and trained with the Royal Signals. Early on, he'd been posted to Italy as a despatch rider; a hazardous job, but seemingly one he was revelling in, if the few letters she'd received were anything to go by.

Seeing him off had been difficult enough, but sending her children away to goodness knows where had nearly broken her heart. She knew she had to do it or risk their safety. They'd gone, with many others; filling the trains with excited chatter; unperturbed by this strange turn of events and looking forward to the adventure. Most were totally oblivious to their mothers sobbing into their hankies and fearing they may never see their precious offspring again.

The end of shift hooter sounded and the women downed tools and switched off their machines as they had done hours earlier. Filing out into the early morning, there was cheerful banter, despite the drama of the night before. As Lizzie grabbed her bicycle, she heard her close friend Freda.

"Hey Lizzie, I've got some sausages from Bert – fancy coming over for your tea?"

The thought of sausages (or any meat for that matter) tempted Lizzie, but she didn't want to intrude on her friend's recent relationship with the local butcher, so thanked her and jokingly said, "Thanks, but I need to wash my hair and do my nails."

"Really?" her friend retorted. "Are you having an affair with someone you haven't told me about?"

"No, in truth, I just need to sleep – I'm so tired. I'll see you tomorrow."

The women waved and went their separate ways.

Lizzie rounded the corner to her street with fear and trepidation, having passed many ruined shops and houses that had been standing the day before. Amazingly, there was little damage and she heaved a sigh of relief as she opened her front door. Everything looked exactly as she'd left it; everything in its place. She liked order and the dishes from her last meal were washed and her bed was made. She undressed mechanically and got in between the cool sheets, not bothering to wash or clean her teeth.

She was woken by a loud rapping on her front door. Rousing from a deep, dreamless sleep, she staggered down the stairs to find the postman on her doorstep with a parcel. Blearily thanking him, she took it through to the kitchen. She looked at the writing on the label. She didn't recognise it, but it was clearly addressed to her.

Thoughtfully, wondering who had sent her a present, she filled the kettle and lit the gas stove before carefully untying the knotted string and unwrapping the brown paper. She gasped as soon as she saw what was inside. A little hand-knitted teddy bear; its beady eyes staring helplessly up at her. This was Ted, who her mother-in-law had made for her daughter, Eve, when she was born and they'd not been apart since. Lizzie felt slightly giddy with a sense of apprehension and tears pricked her eyes as she looked through what else was in the package.

There was an envelope with her name on it in the same handwriting as on the parcel. Fumbling, she opened it to find a letter, clearly enclosing recognisable works of art from her children. The tears flowed then and she wiped them away with a tea towel as she desperately tried to focus.

Vron Cottage, Abergele, North Wales

Dear Mrs Palmer

I am writing to let you know that Billy and Eve have come to stay with me and are settling in well. They were most insistent on sending you this information as soon as possible so you wouldn't worry about them and Eve has sent her precious bear to keep you company.

I hope you receive this letter soon and can respond to them – it would mean so much. Meanwhile, be rest assured I will do all I can to keep them safe and well until they can return home.

Yours sincerely,
Marjorie Bennett

Billy had written in his untidy scrawl:

Dear Mum

Hope your alright and not missing us too much. It's nice here – Mrs Bennett is very kind and looking after us. Eve has only wet the bed once and has stopped crying. We will be going to school soon. I hope you like my picture.

Love you Billy x

Lizzie dried her eyes and couldn't help smile when she saw his drawing of a tree with birds and a squirrel in its branches. This was most unexpected as Billy would normally only draw a train or a plane! A warm, fuzzy feeling enveloped her very soul, knowing her children were safe and in good hands. Inevitably, the tears trickled again when she saw her daughter's naïve drawing of a very smiley cat with huge whiskers and long tail. Framing the page were many love-hearts and at the bottom, 'I love you Mum' and many 'kisses'.

Lizzie carefully smoothed out the paper and read the letters again. This is what she needed to keep her going; to help her endure the hideousness of working in the factory and the nightly air raids.

She made herself a cup of tea and found some bread to toast. She had little food, which hadn't really mattered as she'd had no appetite. Now she had something to live for; a reason to survive. She took the tea and toast back to bed, thinking she might get a few more hours' sleep before getting ready for her next shift, but instead of sleeping, she got up and boiled the kettle again for hot water to bathe in and wash her hair. She would write a note to her children and post it to them.

The air raids during the next few nights were more prolonged; the clear skies giving the enemy more opportunities. All the girls in the factory were war-weary and many found it hard to focus on what they were doing.

Recognising the possible dangers of this situation during the first world war, hostels had been set up in the countryside to offer much-needed respite, away from the constant bombardment of the inner cities. These facilities were being made available again and two or three women at a time were sent for a couple of weeks to recuperate. A rota was drawn up, but with flexibility, ensuring those who needed it the most were given the first available place. These women contributed so much to the war effort, just as men on the front line. They'd made sacrifices and every day faced the very real probability of losing their lives.

Lizzie was coping better than most and had willingly given up her slot on more than one occasion, but eventually the foreman had called her into his office and said, "Take a break Lizzie, you've earned it."

Lizzie wasn't sure she wanted to leave her home, not even for a week. In truth, she was afraid to go in case there was nothing left when she got back. It was an irrational fear as her house could be destroyed whether she was there or not, yet somehow it felt as though she was deserting her position of responsibility; the place where one day she would welcome back her family.

"Where am I going?"

"To a place in North Wales."

TAKE THREE

Sipping my first cup of coffee and waiting for my decadent breakfast of scrambled eggs and smoked salmon, I notice a young man standing awkwardly at the doorway, waiting to be seated. His dark hair is tousled and his shirt and trousers are rumpled, as though he's slept in them – perhaps he has. He's wearing thick, dark-rimmed glasses and I can see, even from where I'm sitting, he looks pale and anxious. He doesn't have long to remain in the limelight and the waitress shows him to a table adjacent to mine.

"Good morning," I say.

I get a nod in response. I can see he bites his nails and doesn't wear socks. I wonder what he's doing here? He's totally oblivious to my scrutiny and resorts to stabbing at his phone.

There's a flurry of activity as the boldest, brightest jumpsuit on high heels is ushered to a table by the window where she flounces into a chair, dumping an enormous handbag on one of the others.

"Just grapefruit, toast and coffee dear," she says to the waitress in an overly loud, posh voice, "I have to watch my figure."

I don't agree, somewhat enviously, as I would say she's no more than a size 8. She fiddles with the beads that are colour-coordinated with her pink and purple outfit, and stares out the window. There's not much to see as a mist has come in, so she turns her attention to her long-painted nails before attempting to engage in conversation with the gentleman at the next table.

"Rather murky out there," she says, stating the obvious.

"Not very nice," the gentleman responds as he gets up to leave.

The lady resorts to shaking out her napkin and pouring coffee, looking disappointed that their encounter had been so brief.

I'm distracted by my breakfast being served and when I look across again, the lady is spooning grapefruit into her mouth as though she's sucking lemons, clearly prepared to suffer for fashion.

A couple are shown to the table between me and tousle-head. They don't look like a conventional couple as there's very obviously an age gap. Maybe they're father and daughter, but I don't think so, judging by her 'doey-eyes' never leaving his face. He's tall, grey and handsome; she's dark-haired and petite, wearing little make-up and looks about sixteen. They order breakfast and even though they're within earshot, I can't hear what they're saying. The body language is difficult to read. She's clearly besotted, but he's just being polite in a fatherly kind of way. They're barely speaking above a whisper. How odd. He doesn't look like a sex trafficker, but then she doesn't look old enough to have left school, never mind be away from home.

I've finished my breakfast and leave at the same time as tousle-head, who politely stands aside for me to go through the door first and I can't help notice that he smells good, which is really weird, given the rest of his appearance.

A final glance at the lady and see she's staring out of the window again, no doubt longing for her prince to come.

THE GIRL ON THE BUS

The bus stops with a puff of brakes and the doors open, allowing passengers to alight, before those of us waiting patiently, can get on. I shuffle forward instinctively as the queue shortens and when I hear the driver say, "Mind how you go," I know to step up and present my pass.

"Good morning, Sir," the driver says cheerily, "and how are you today?"

"Well, thank you," I reply and make my way to the nearest empty seat.

I've been catching the same bus every weekday for years to get to my job in town and nearly every day it's the same helpful driver. The doors close, then reopen and I hear a breathless voice say, "Oh thank you, you've saved my life! I couldn't be late today." Money rattles into the fare machine, the doors close and I feel someone taking the seat beside me.

"I was cutting that fine," says a girl's voice, "I've got an interview and couldn't decide what to wear!"

"I'm sure you've made the right choice," I say, "What's the job?"

"Shop assistant in the Ladies Fashion Department in Debenhams. I need some work experience before starting University. I want to be a fashion designer."

The girl's enthusiasm is obvious and her openness like a breath of fresh air.

"I can see why you'd like to get this job; it could be useful."

"Park Parade," the driver calls out.

"This is my stop; I'm afraid I'll have to disturb you."

My companion moves out of her seat and I grab my white stick saying, "Good luck, I hope you're successful."

"Thank you," comes the reply.

I give the incident little more thought until I'm standing in the queue the next day and idly wonder how the girl on the bus got on.

I'm exchanging pleasantries with the driver when I hear footsteps and a breathless voice saying, "Nearly late again!"

"How did you get on?" I ask.

"I got it and start today!"

"I'm delighted for you - well done."

The voice continues to chatter animatedly as we make our way to two empty seats. When she draws breath, I reach out my hand and introduce myself. She returns the compliment and says her name is Marcie.

We meet at the bus stop all summer. Marcie is rarely late and I look forward to hearing about her encounters at work, which are often very amusing. One day she says sadly, "Paul, this is my last day. I'm going to Uni next week."

"I'll miss you," I say sincerely, "my mornings won't be the same without our chat."

"Can I keep in touch somehow," she asks, "maybe by 'phone?"

We've never mentioned my blindness, so I'm overwhelmed by her thoughtfulness and whilst I would enjoy nothing more, I don't want her to feel obliged. I'm certain that once she gets settled at university, our daily natters will become a thing of the past. However, she insists on taking my number and I'm touched when she squeezes my arm and says, "Take care of yourself," as we say goodbye.

She calls a couple of times, sounding excited about her new life and when I thank her for taking the trouble, she responds by saying, "It's good to talk."

Winter sets in and it's sometimes cold and miserable waiting at the bus stop. Regular passengers pass the time of day, but no more than that. It's Christmas Eve and I'm on the bus, showing my pass, when I hear the sound of Marcie's feet.

"Better hang on a minute," I say to the driver, "I think we've got a latecomer."

I stand aside as Marcie steps onto the platform. "Hello Marcie - you just made it."

"How on earth did you know it was me?" Marcie exclaims incredulously.

"Intuition," I respond as we take our seats.

Marcie is back at Debenhams and we chat incessantly until we hear, "Park Parade" and I get out of my seat. I feel her hand on my arm and an impulsive kiss on my lips. "Merry Christmas," she says.

"Merry Christmas," I reply choking with emotion as I leave the bus. A cold wind brings tears to my eyes and their saltiness mingles with the taste of her lipstick.

THE HAG STONE

The water swirls around my ankles and the grainy sand shifts beneath my feet. I'm looking out to the horizon and the pale glow of dawn.

A wave splashes against my shins and the spray reaches my shorts, but I don't move. I keep staring out to sea; marvelling at its vastness and fascinated by the seamless join between sea and sky. Clouds scud over the water, casting rippled shadows.

The tide is turning and the wind strengthening; my hair blows across my face, obscuring my view. I take a step and turn my head, looking in another direction. Rocks, slick with lichen, lean jaggedly at the water's edge. I make my way towards them, slowly dragging my bare feet through the shallows.

This beach, mostly shingle and pebbles, only reveals a thin strip of gravelly sand at low tide. I wade through a small pool; tangled seaweed restricting my progress. A much larger wave crashes onto shore; spitting surf much further up the beach. The tide is coming in quickly and I should retreat. Instead, I continue to head for the rocky outcrop, from where I'll be able to climb up and onto a footpath.

The sky is darkening and I hear a rumble of thunder in the distance; a sudden flash of lightening briefly lights up the sky. A storm is coming, but I don't hurry. Carefully picking my way to the nearest rock, I sit down and retrieve the trainers tied by their laces around my neck. Picking off the tendrils of seaweed and brushing the sand from my soles, I slip my feet into the shoes. As I'm tying the laces, I notice a small, flat grey stone poking out of the shingle and pick it up. I marvel at its smoothness and strange shape; two perfect holes slightly off-centre, seemingly grotesque; empty eyes in a haggard face.

'A witch's stone,' I murmur, 'a lucky charm that's supposed to save lives.'

I put the stone in my pocket and begin the climb. The rocks are rough and slippery; my trainers lose their grip and send me sprawling; my hands grapple for something to stop my fall; there is nothing and my face smacks into the unrelenting surface as I slither downwards, scraping my shins. I feel the water lapping around my waist and vainly reach up to climb again. Thunder is crashing overhead now and visibility is poor. I decide to return to the beach. My clothes are saturated and my shoes filled with water as I cautiously make my way around the base of the rocks. Suddenly, I'm engulfed by a gigantic wave and painfully winded when I'm smashed against the rocks. I can do nothing to resist the power of the sea as it sucks me into its depths. I am gone.

"Hello, can you hear me?" a voice says.

I feel a hand on my wrist, another behind my head and again the voice, "Can you hear me?" Then, "He's coming round, thank goodness, that was a close thing."

My head hurts and I can't focus, but I remember what happened. Surely, I can't still be alive?

"Hello," the voice says again, "I'm a Paramedic and you're one very lucky chap. Welcome back!"

Gently I'm lifted onto a stretcher; the storm has abated, but it's still raining. As I'm carried up the beach to the ambulance, I furtively reach into my pocket. The stone is still there; the hag stone that undoubtedly saved my life.

THE PATH LEADING HOME

It had been blustery all day with intermittent showers, keeping the children mostly indoors, but the sound of a bell clanging sent them scurrying for their coats. Emma, running into the kitchen, could see her mother in the garden wrestling with the washing. She took a couple of crusts from the bread bin and an apple from the fruit bowl and got to the front door at the same time as her little brother Jack. They pulled on their wellington boots and let themselves out of the house.

As they ran down the lane, they heard the bell again, louder this time and accompanied by the familiar cry, "Rag and bone - any old iron!" They quickened their pace until they reached the big road where they stopped, slightly out of breath.

"We made it," gasped Emma.

The bell kept ringing and now they could hear the slow clip-clop of horse's hooves on tarmac. Around the bend in the road came the sight they were waiting for and they waved enthusiastically. A covered wagon, pulled by a sturdy black and white horse was plodding towards them. As it drew level, the horse's ears pricked expectantly and Paddy smiled at the children, who were nearly always there waiting for him, no matter when he came or what the weather.

"Hello you two, what have you got for Barney today?"

"Bread and an apple," Emma replied and gave the horse a pat before holding out one of the crusts. Jack wasn't so brave and stood back watching.

"Here Jack - give him a crust - he won't bite!"

Tentatively, Jack stretched out his arm, holding as little of the bread as he could without dropping it. As soon as the horse's muzzle touched it, Jack snatched his hand away as the morsel disappeared.

To Jack, who was only four, the animal seemed enormous. Emma loved horses and although they lived on a farm, she had yet to persuade her parents to buy her one, so she was always delighted when Paddy and Barney came through their village.

Emma gave Barney the apple and he tossed his head, sending saliva and juice showering over them!

"Err," Jack said disgustedly and retreated further. Emma laughed and gave Barney another pat.

"Like a ride?" Paddy asked them.

"Yes please," replied Emma without hesitation and before he could refuse, she'd hoisted Jack up beside Paddy and clambered up behind him.

"You best get in the back," Paddy said in his gentle Irish accent, "it'll be safer."

The children scrambled obediently inside the wagon, doing their best to avoid getting tangled up with the various bits of scrap and old clothes.

The wagon jolted as Barney pulled away and they heard Paddy say, "Trot on Barney." The sound of quickening hooves added to their excitement and even though they couldn't see where they were going, they were enjoying the ride and couldn't stop smiling.

They felt Barney slow to a walk and Paddy said, "I'd better drop you off here or your mum will be wondering where you are."

The wagon stopped and the children clambered down to the road.

"Thank you so much! What do you say Jack?" Emma prompted.

"Thank you," Jack said still beaming.

They waved goodbye as the wagon set off again and, it wasn't until it was almost out of sight, that Emma realised she had absolutely no idea where they were! They didn't often go out of the village, except on the school bus and she didn't know this place at all. Surrounded by high hedges on either side, Emma could see nowhere familiar.

Not wanting to alarm Jack, she said, "Right, best we get home before mum comes looking for us."

Emma was eight and a bright child. She knew she should've checked with their mother before leaving the road end, but the opportunity had been too good to miss and surely, they couldn't be that far away?

She set off determinedly, in the opposite direction to the way the wagon was heading, with Jack running to keep up. A little way along the road, Emma noticed a bridge and ran on to it, hoping to see somewhere she recognised. As she stood on tiptoes and peered over the wall, she could just make out a cinder track below.

"Come on Jack," she said cheerily, "there's a path under this bridge. That'll be the way back home."

Together they slithered down the bank and taking Jack's hand, Emma strode out confidently.

They'd been walking a while when Jack stopped. With a quivering lip and blinking back tears he said, "I want to go home Em - it's getting dark and I'm hungry."

Trying to sound positive Emma coaxed her little brother to keep walking. "We can't be far away now - let's do marching." With that she set off again singing at the top of her voice, "The grand old Duke of York, he had ten thousand men, he marched them up to the top of the hill and he marched them down again!"

Jack joined in and after several renditions with Emma doing actions and Jack trying to copy, they were still nowhere familiar and it really was getting dark.

Emma was beginning to feel desperate when she saw a faint light just ahead of them. "Come on Jack, there's a light, we must be near the village."

As they drew closer, they could see through the shadows a small cottage, raised on a platform. Emma realised then, they'd been following the disused railway line and this was the old station.

Without thinking, she ran up to the door and knocked on it loudly. Barking could be heard in response and a voice saying, "Quiet Meg." The door opened a crack, "Who is it?"

"Emma and Jack and we're lost. Can you please help us?"

The door opened wider to reveal an old man in braces with a bushy grey beard and horn-rimmed spectacles peering at them in astonishment.

"Where've you come from? How did you get here?"

Emma explained what had happened and the old man was quick to reassure them and invite them in. The collie they'd heard barking sidled out of her bed waving her tail in welcome.

It was very dark inside, lit only by a reading lamp. The old man moved a tabby cat out of the only armchair and disappeared into a back room, reappearing moments later with glasses of milk and biscuits. The children gratefully accepted the snack whilst the man telephoned the Police to get them home as quickly as possible.

Somehow, they'd managed to walk beyond the village and were actually heading in the wrong direction! The ride in a police car certainly added to the day's adventures and although their mother had been frantic, she was too relieved to be cross with them and almost squeezed the breath out of them with her hugs. They solemnly promised they would never to go off like that again, but missed seeing Paddy and Barney, who didn't come through their village any more.

THE PRICE OF LIFE

I sit alone in the hospital cafeteria, staring blindly into my coffee cup. I'm barely aware of the people around me, but can't ignore what is being said at the next table.

"What was it the Consultant said?"

"It's terminal Mum, there's nothing more they can do."

"How long?"

"Six to nine months, maybe a year."

I sit staring into my empty cup - my empty life, but at least I have a life. My operation is already scheduled for fourteen long weeks away. I can change my mind at any time before then, but it will have to be before; any time after, is the point of no return. Another conversation invades my thoughts.

"When's the due date?"

"19th May. I'm *so* excited and I can't wait to tell Geoff."

"I'm not sure he'll be as thrilled as you obviously are."

"Why do you say that Mum?"

"Because he's married and already has a family!"

"So? He loves me and he'll love this baby. Please Mum don't spoil it!"

"I'm sorry, but you have to face facts and be prepared to make difficult decisions. He hasn't left his wife; he doesn't live with you and I bet you haven't even discussed having a baby with him, have you?"

"No, but he'll be fine with it honestly and if he isn't, well I'll have to cross that bridge when I come to it."

Cross that bridge? I wish I could take a step back. I'm so sorry. It's all my fault. I recognised the rash as soon as I saw it and even though I suspected I was pregnant; I wasn't concerned at all! I've been in contact with German measles many times without getting infected and always assumed I was immune. How wrong could I be? How careless; how stupid!

"You've been careless and stupid and you can't just wait to see what'll happen and hope for the best! A baby isn't just for Christmas!

I continue to stare into my empty cup, squeezing the tears back behind my eyelids and trying to ignore the rising lump in my throat that threatens to burst out in a howl. I hear quiet sobbing and gentle, soothing words.

"I'm so sorry Mum. I wish it could have been better news, but you have to try and stay strong and make the most of whatever time you have left together. Dad seems positive - he won't give up without a fight and you mustn't either."

"I know, I'm being selfish, but life without your dad won't be a life. I just can't imagine it. We've spent over fifty years together with hardly a day apart - whatever will I do?"

Whatever will I do?

"You'll carry on as normally as possible.

Carry on normally; is that even possible?

"Once they've got his meds sorted out, he can be discharged and it'll be up to you to make him comfortable and happy at home. Don't give up on him Mum. Miracles do happen and if only you can stay positive, it'll help Dad."

I need a miracle.

"Have faith in me Mum."

"I just want what's best for you; and the baby."

"I know you do, but you have to trust me."

Trust me? Trust me to do the right thing when the right thing feels so very wrong. Contracting the virus so early in pregnancy will more than likely result in my baby being born with abnormalities and the advice is to terminate.

Ultimately, the choice can only be mine; to keep this little life or let it go.

THE YEAR 2020

Twenty-twenty sounded so special; extravagantly celebrated with firework displays all around the world. Cities everywhere, lit up by their brightness. In London, Big Ben, having been silenced for restoration, struck the familiar resounding dongs at midnight. This was the joyful and promising start to a new year; a new decade.

Any euphoria was short-lived as bush fires raged across continents; unstoppable; destroying people's homes and the habitats of wildlife. Vast swathes of land were left scorched and black; animals, unable to escape, perished. Early evacuation saved lives in populated places, but many were left homeless, their treasured possessions gone.

Then came rumours from the East that an unknown and lethal virus was spreading through China, taking many lives. We watched, fascinated, by TV footage showing people wearing masks, whilst attempting to go about their daily lives. Somehow it didn't seem that threatening or dangerous to the west, but within weeks COVID-19 had reached Europe and the UK.

Lockdowns were imposed in an effort to contain the disease. Elderly people were warned they could be particularly susceptible and anyone with underlying health conditions, should self-isolate. The advice to everyone was to stay at home to save lives and help the NHS cope with the likely pandemic. Such was the urgency and predictability this would happen, that many patients, due to receive treatment or surgery, had their schedules cancelled.

Masks weren't thought to be beneficial. Social distancing, washing hands regularly and self-isolation for those at risk or showing symptoms, was deemed sufficient. Despite these precautions, the virus spread; most acutely among the elderly in nursing homes. Some of these patients had been discharged from hospital, without being tested for COVID, to free up beds for the expected influx. Inevitably, coronavirus became rife in these residences and many died.

Personal protection equipment was in short supply and unavoidably, some health professionals succumbed. Testing was slow to get started and it was even slower to get results. Intensive care beds were full and the most severely affected were put on ventilators.

The biggest concern was that some people could be asymptomatic, having no indication they carried the disease, and they could infect others without realising. Hospital staff worked tirelessly to manage the situation, but it was feared the epidemic would get worse and the Army was drafted in to create field hospitals, named after Florence Nightingale.

Testing was sporadic and not easily available. Results were still slow to materialise, thus leaving potential carriers in limbo, wondering whether or not to isolate.

Schools closed and so did most public places, except for essential suppliers, such as supermarkets. They put one-way systems in place and limited how many customers could enter the store. Still no masks, but this approach seemed to be helping to reduce the spread. There was panic buying; mainly toilet rolls and sanitising products, and stores had to limit each customer to only three items of any product.

These restrictions were accepted by the majority, but as the weeks rolled on, inevitably there were some who became rebellious and threatened the health of others. An incident that seemed to trigger this excuse was when a black man in America died when he was being detained by Police. Within hours, a campaign went world-wide proclaiming that 'Black Lives Matter'. *All* lives matter and the resulting consequences from these protests were shocking. People were injured and Police were overwhelmed.

Neighbourhoods were united in their appreciation of all front-line workers and public applause became a weekly ritual every Thursday evening.

Politicians and scientists couldn't agree on the best procedures, so the Nations became divided, each having different regulations, making lives complicated. Ministers and advisers to the Government failed to adhere to their own advice, which led to severe criticism.

Eventually, schools re-opened and students returned to university, even though much of their learning was still being conducted on-line. Inevitably, some of these youngsters tested positive and had to self-isolate.

Efforts were made to boost the economy by relaxing laws, but in some places, lockdown had to be implemented again when cases of coronavirus increased. Elsewhere households were permitted to meet outside within certain numbers, depending on where they lived, but not indoors, although they could meet in a café! It made little sense.

2020 will be historically remembered as another 'Annus Mirabilis'. The first year designated with this title was 1666 when Londoners suffered the Great Plague followed by the Great Fire. Despite modern scientific research and predicted global warming, seemingly no lessons have been learnt in the last three hundred and fifty-four years to prevent it all happening again and, without 20/20 vision, we have little way of knowing what will happen in the future.

THE POEMS

My poetry is often inspired by life events and
attributed to my family. I like it to rhyme, which is
considered somewhat old fashioned, but to me,
that's what makes it poetry!

MEMORIES

Some memories fade

Through the mists of time

But many linger on

We remember the good times

As well as the bad

We smile at the happy

And cry at the sad

Thoughts come to mind

Through vision and sound

Clouds in the sky

Leaves on the ground

A favourite song

A familiar face

A certain scent

A special place

Memories shine through like a bright star

And make you the person you truly are

A DAY TO REMEMBER

Recalling memories of the fight
When sirens sounded day and night
Silence then filled the air
Bringing joy and hope; no more despair

Battles won and battles lost
Now is the time to count the cost
Of those brave souls who set us free
To live again in liberty

Peace has prevailed for all these years
And we'll remember through our tears
The songs, the stories we hold dear
We will remember them

ALONE IN THE SNOW

A pure white blanket covers the ground;
A robin sings shrilly as I look around.
My footsteps don't falter, I know where to go;
I know where I'll find you alone in the snow.

I follow the footpath lined by the trees;
Old oaks and sycamores bent by the breeze.
I see you now as you patiently wait,
'I'm coming,' I call as I go through the gate.

You sit on our bench; not moving, so still;
Did you not hear me? Do you not feel the chill?
Is it not you? I can't see your face,
But I remembered the time and our special place.

I give you a wave as I hurry on;
So nearly there, but where have you gone?
I sit on our bench and I don't really know
How I came to be here, alone in the snow.

I CRADLE YOU GENTLY

I cradle you gently
Watching you sleep
So peaceful, so perfect
I silently weep

Holding you closer
Not letting go
My arms full of love
You'll never know

No rhyme nor reason
To lose you my son
Ripped from my womb
Before life has begun

My heart's breaking
But I don't want to cry
As I cradle you gently
And kiss you goodbye

IF YOU CAN SEE A RAINBOW

If you can see a rainbow
When the storm is done
It'll only be a moment
Before you see the sun

Thunder clouds roll away
To leave a clear blue sky
Then appears a rainbow
Uniting you and I

When you're in that moment
You share the rainbow too
Believe it's awesome magic
And make your dreams come true

Look beyond the rainbow
And further than the moon
Trust in God's help to save us
From all this doom and gloom

MY WALK

Empty streets, deserted park
No other sound except the lark
Passed fields of ripening wheat
Ewes, their lambs with plaintive bleat
Horses, cattle quietly grazing
These country scenes are so amazing

Beyond the town, the castle's stood
Beside a lake within a wood
Swan's beating wings, ducks waddle and quack
Sweet scented garlic beside the track
A glimpse of a squirrel or even a deer
Lost to the forest as I draw near

Twittering birds and croaking frogs
Few walkers with their lively dogs
Dappled sunlight, trickling stream
Heathered hills, valleys green
All these pictures of where I roam
I take with me as I head home

RETURN TO THE RIDINGS

The skirl of pipes and beat of drums
Clattering hooves as the Reiver comes
With his Lass, they parade the Square
Cheers from the crowd gathered there

Leading the pageant in swirling kilts
The band marches to haunting lilts
Return to the ridings along the borders
Defending the town against marauders

'To Duns Law' the Reiver cried
Where blood's been spilt and many've died
Away up the hill, gallop the steeds
Reiver's men taking the lead

They stop at the top to take in the view
This land of clans claimed by the few
Rituals passed down from father to son
Stories told how battles were won

Strangers are welcome and peace will remain
Until they return to the ridings again

THE SEASONS

Winter wraps the land in snow
From mountain tops to valleys below
Silvery forests; frozen lakes
Carpets of snowdrops; the year awakes

Daffodils herald the coming of Spring
New life; new growth; new everything
Fields of yellow; hedgerows green
Twittering birds; babbling stream

Summer's warmth; blue sky, calm sea
Sweet smelling blossom; humming bee
A shady glade; ripening corn
A rousing chorus before the dawn

Burnished leaves of red and gold
Swirling winds; strong and cold
Autumn mists; fading sun
Dying days; the year is done

# UNDER THE SUMMER SUN

Across golden sands, a blue sea glistens
Under the summer sun
Its warmth is very welcome
Now that winter's done
Waders - birds and people
Tiptoe to water's edge
Shrieking in mock protest
When cold waves slap their legs
Braver souls venture further in,
Some wearing wet suits,
To surf or to swim
Distantly, a tanker glides by
A speck on the ocean
Between sea and sky
Nearer to shore, guarding the bay
A lighthouse warns sailors
'Don't come this way'
Along the beach, families having fun
Playing games, enjoying picnics
Under the summer sun

TECHNOLOGY

I remember when girls and boys
Played with dolls, trains and other toys
Climbing trees, flying kites
Roller skating, riding bikes
Now with games on X-Box and Wii
There's barely any time for tea!

Years ago, we had only radio
'Listen with Mother' our favourite show
Then came TV with a tiny screen
Witness the Coronation of our Queen
Men on the moon, rockets to the stars
Exploring the universe and life on Mars

Affecting our lives every day
We've learnt new skills along the way
PC, laptop, iPad or phone
Fit Bit, tablet, camera or drone
How would we cope, where would we be?
Without Information Technology!

HOLD MY HAND

"Hold my hand," said sister Kate
As she led me through the garden gate
"Where are we going?" I want to know
"Hush, it's a secret, just don't let go!"

She took me to the railway track
And I could tell there was no going back
"I want to go home," I begin to whine
"Oh come on Jack, you'll be fine!"

A few more steps and I come to a halt
"If we get in trouble, it's all your fault!"
"We won't," she says, "just keep walking
And save your breath with a little less talking!"

We wander on until it's almost dark
And then I hear a familiar bark
"We must be near Granny's house," I say with glee
"We are," Kate says, "and in time for tea!"

ONE BRIEF MOMENT IN TIME

A cool summer breeze
Stirs the grass in the meadow
Birds sing and bees hum

The scent of roses
Pleasantly pervades the air
Bright blooms of colour

The warmth of the sun
Finds even the shady spots
Beneath the tall trees

The sound of water
Cascading from a fountain
Dragon flies dancing

Pure fluffy white clouds
Scud over a clear blue sky
Beyond distant hills

Marching ants in line
Along cracks and crevices
In the sturdy garden wall

A cat sleeps soundly
As a blackbird looks for worms
Oblivious to danger

A snail's trail shiny
Along the path to the door
Marking an amazing journey

WHAT IS A LIFE?

What is a life?
A passage in time
A step, a milestone
Along the line

What is a life?
A voyage through years
Excitement, happiness
Sadness and fears

What is a life?
An adventure each day
Hopes, dreams and promises
Paving the way

What is a life?
How can it be measured?
A journey to eternity
Every moment treasured

Author's Biography

Chris has written everything from poetry to pantomime. It took her ten years to complete her memoirs and having been a member of several inspirational writing groups, derives great pleasure from completing assignments and sharing efforts. She is writing her second novel and has regularly submitted articles, poems and short stories to magazines, radio and the talking newspaper.

Printed in Great Britain
by Amazon

17614078R10068